SHAKA
WARRIOR KING OF THE
ZULU

by
LYNN BEDFORD HALL

Illustrations by
RENÉ HERMANS

Contents

STRUIK

An unhappy childhood

It was a blistering hot day at the height of summer. The sun beat down out of a cloudless sky, and the veld shimmered and shrivelled in the heat. A young woman called Nandi strode swiftly along a narrow, stony track. Holding her hand, and trying desperately to keep up, was her six-year-old son. His name was Shaka, and on this particular morning he was as unhappy as any child could possibly be. He had been sobbing for hours, and his tears had left shiny wet paths on his dusty cheeks. He was also very frightened, and kept looking back over his shoulder as they walked.

"Mother," he whimpered, "I did not see that wild dog creeping up to my father's sheep. I was not asleep! I was sitting under a tree throwing stones at a lizard. I did not see the dog until he pounced and tore the sheep to pieces! Why is my father so cross with me over one little sheep when he has so many? Why has he sent us away?"

Sadly Nandi shook her head. She knew why her husband, Chief Senzangakhona, had never shown much love for her and their son Shaka. It was because she belonged to the Qwabe clan, who were not supposed to marry with the Zulu. There had been no royal wedding, although as a princess she was entitled to one. Because she was expecting Senzangakhona's baby, she simply became his third wife, and was not at all welcomed by the rest of his people.

Nandi sighed quietly to herself as she walked. Even though she knew she was unpopular, she never dreamed that her husband would go so far as to drive them away from his kraal – and all because of one small sheep.

"Never mind, my little lion cub," she said to her son, squeezing his hand tightly. "We shall return to my father's people, the Langeni. You will make many friends there, and we will both be happy."

Shaka's eyes brightened at this piece of news. He was tired of being teased and taunted by the other boys at his father's kraal.

"Perhaps I will find some good companions among my mother's people," he thought. He reached over and patted the head of the baby his mother carried on her back.

"Nomcoba, my little sister, you are still too small to know about these things," he said, "but we will take good care of you."

Little did Shaka know that he would be unhappier than ever in his new home. Although he was only six, he was immediately made a herd-boy, and he spent his days in the veld, looking after the sheep and cattle. The other herd-boys were unfriendly and cruel to him. More than anything else, they loved to torment him about his name, which means 'beetle'.

"Hah!" they shouted, dancing around Shaka and pointing their fingers at him. "Ah-ha, Shaka, you poor little beetle, nobody wants you and your loud-mouthed mother here. Son of a chief? Hah! Why are you not in his kraal then? Go home and take your mother with you – she who shrills with a voice like a cricket."

Some of the older bullies took great delight in forcing Shaka to lick boiling hot porridge off a wooden spoon. At other times they shouted, "Hold out your hands, beetle!" and into his cupped palms they ladled boiling stew. "If you drop any we will pull your wrinkled ears off!"

But Shaka was too tough to cry. All the teasing and bullying had made him proud and cheeky. He realized that the only way he could get the better of his tormentors was to become stronger and more powerful than any of them.

"Soon I will show these cowards what this little beetle can do," he promised himself fiercely. "And they will be sorry for what they said about me and my mother!"

Shaka also knew that he could always find comfort with Nandi.

"Ah, my little fire," she said after one of his fights, wagging her finger at him. "You must take no notice of those jealous jackals. Look at me." Shaka stared up at his mother with big brown eyes. "Nandi knows that you are going to be a great chief one day," she told him. "You will be greater than the rising sun and stronger than a great bull elephant. I can feel it in my bones, my son."

The man who gave his name to a nation

Many hundreds of years ago, a boy was born to a woman called Nozinja, who lived in what is now known as Zululand, or KwaZulu. Although Nozinja had many children, this boy was her favourite, and she decided to give him a very special name – Zulu – which means 'sky'. One of Zulu's brothers, Qwabe, became very jealous of him, and plotted to kill him. When Zulu's mother heard of this plot, she took him to live in another part of the country. Here, Zulu grew up to be a powerful man and eventually founded the Zulu clan, to which Shaka's ancestors belonged. When Shaka was a boy, the Zulu were a small and unimportant clan of about two thousand people.

The young warrior

Some years later, a terrible drought ravaged the land. The rivers all dried up, the crops withered and died, and people were forced to eat roots and wild plants to survive. Nandi decided to send Shaka to live with an aunt amongst the Mthethwa people, where there was enough food for everyone. At last Shaka found himself in a clan who treated him kindly, and the headman of the kraal welcomed him as one of his herd-boys. Shaka was now sixteen, and had grown into a tall, strong and proud young man. He soon became the leader of his group of herd-boys, and because he was a senior, was allowed to wear a leather girdle around his waist and a soft skin apron. He was also given several light spears and a black shield made of cow hide.

Each herd-boy also carried a bundle of sharp sticks, with which they played their favourite game. A round fleshy root or melon, about the size of a small football, was sent rolling down a steep, bumpy slope while the boys stood some distance away and threw their sticks at the moving target. Once a boy could spear a root or melon, he could easily kill rabbits and small buck in exactly the same way. Shaka's group always won the games because he had trained them so well.

Of course, playing in the veld could be dangerous, and the herd-boys had to keep a constant look-out for snakes and the wild animals which often threatened their herds. One day they spotted a leopard in a tree.

"Let us call the men!" the boys shouted, running away in terror. "They will come and kill the leopard! Run, Shaka, run!"

But Shaka ignored their screams. He grabbed two spears and a stout club and walked slowly towards the animal. Taking careful aim, he hurled a spear at the leopard. The point of the blade pierced its shoulder, and snarling with rage and pain, it leapt down out of the tree and charged towards Shaka. Without flinching, he quickly plunged his second spear into the leopard's chest, and with an almighty blow of his club crushed its skull. When the men arrived on the scene they were astounded by his courage.

"You are indeed a brave young man!" they said to Shaka. "The king will be very pleased when you take him the skin of this leopard."

Shaka felt very proud when he was awarded his first cow for bravery. How he wished that the boys who had bullied him so mercilessly as a child could see him now!

"They would not dare mock this little beetle now!" he muttered to himself. "I, Shaka, am stronger and braver than any one of those boastful weaklings."

Not long afterwards, Jobe, the king of the Mthethwa, died and was succeeded by his son Dingiswayo. As a young man, Dingiswayo had roamed all over the country. He had seen how guns were used by the white men and how their troops were trained, and he was determined to build up a powerful army.

Shaka was overjoyed when he was chosen to be one of Dingiswayo's warriors. His regiment had a special uniform: white ox tails, which were worn around the ankles and wrists, a kilt made of strips of fur, a cap of skin with black feathers, and sandals of ox hide. Each soldier was also given a large shield and three spears.

Although Shaka was very popular amongst the other warriors, he was unable to forget his unhappy childhood and spent many hours alone.

"One day those cowardly cockroaches will pay for what they did to me and my mother," he vowed.

Shaka soon proved himself to be a fearless soldier, but he was not happy with the way battles were fought. He thought it stupid that the two armies stood far away from each other, shouting insults and wildly hurling their spears into the enemy ranks.

"They are like a group of toothless old women!" he thought in disgust. "Often they are too afraid to stand close enough to kill each other!" He paced up and down inside his hut, his eyebrows drawn together in fierce concentration. "Is it not foolish to stand and throw our spears into the wind? These spears which break as easily as dry twigs? And these clumsy sandals are nothing but a hindrance! How can a warrior run with such things tied to his feet?

For weeks and weeks he thought about it, and finally he decided what to do.

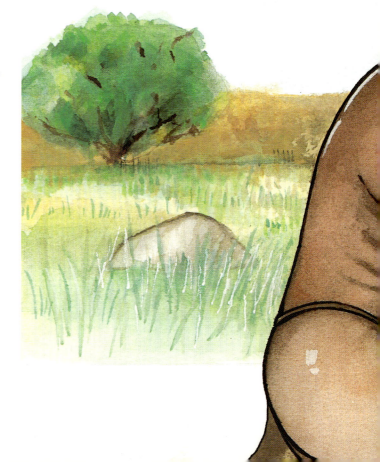

A Zulu kraal

The part of the country in which Shaka lived was studded with thick forests and threaded with rivers and beautiful green valleys. There were, of course, no roads or towns, but all over the countryside little settlements could be seen: circles of round, dome-shaped huts, with doorways so small and low that people had to crawl in on their hands and knees. The floors were made of crushed antheap and clay and smeared with cow dung, which dried as hard as rock. Near the doorway, there was a hollow in the floor for the fire and, to one side, an area where goats and calves could be tied up for the night in bad weather. Each circle of huts was the home of one man, and each hut belonged to one of his wives and her little children. In the centre of everything was a circular enclosure for cattle. The whole settlement was surrounded by a fence of poles, and was called a kraal.

Shaka's new way of fighting

Some distance away, in the middle of a dark, thick forest, lived a well-known blacksmith. One day Shaka went to visit him, and he asked him whether he could make a very special spear – one with a short, heavy shaft and a strong stabbing blade. It had to be perfectly shaped and balanced, made of freshly smelted iron, and dipped into a special brew of heart and liver mixed with fat, to give it magic powers.

"This will be a big task," said the blacksmith when he had listened to Shaka's request. "You will have to pay me well." Shaka agreed to give the blacksmith one calf, and a few weeks later the spear was completed.

Shaka was pleased with his new weapon. It had a sturdy wooden shaft and a blade so sharp that it could shave off the hairs on his arm. He decided that, once it had drawn blood, the spear was to be called *Ixwa*, pronounced 'Iklwa'. Some people think that Shaka chose this word because it sounded just like the sucking noise the blade of a spear made when it was pulled from a victim's flesh.

"If our warriors are armed with these short spears, and if we all go barefoot so that we can run faster than our enemies, we will surely conquer the whole of the land," he told himself.

When the Zulu went to battle against the Buthelezi clan, Shaka was able to put his new weapon to the test. The Buthelezi, who were expecting the usual wild and noisy spear-throwing battle, were astounded when Shaka's regiment marched straight up to them.

"You are only six hundred strong!" they sneered at their enemy. "We have a mighty army. We command you to surrender!"

The Buthelezi laughed in scorn, and their best warrior stepped forward. "Send me your bravest soldier!" he shouted. "Your strongest lion! And I shall carve him up like a piece of rotten fruit."

Without hesitating, Shaka stepped forward. "Come then!" he shouted in a voice like thunder. "Come, you son of a porcupine! You, who shakes like the tail of a mouse! I, Shaka, will show you who is the lion here today!" And with a terrible cry he rushed at the bewildered man, knocked his shield aside and drove his stabbing spear through the defenceless man's body.

"*Ngadla!*" his war-cry echoed in the hills. "*Ngadla!* I have eaten!" Without stopping, Shaka rushed onwards, followed by his two faithful friends, Mgobozi and Ngoboka, and then by the whole of his regiment. In no time the entire Buthelezi army had fled in terror.

"Bring this Shaka to me!" commanded Dingiswayo after the battle. "Let me see this brave warrior!" Later, when Shaka stood before him, Dingiswayo knew instantly that this young man was a great soldier and leader. He decided to promote him immediately.

"You shall be captain of one hundred warriors," he told Shaka, "and I shall also reward you with ten head of cattle."

Shaka trained his group of one hundred men very strictly and with iron discipline. He was determined that his men would become the fastest, strongest and most fearless warriors in the land. They scored one

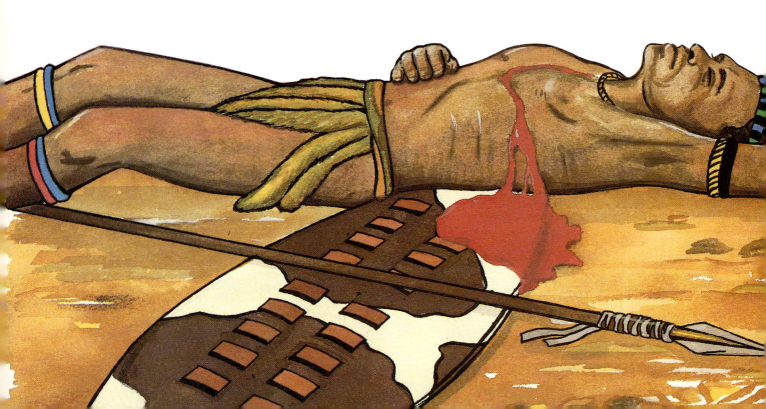

victory after another, following their leader into battle as he shouted his terrible war-cry, "*Si-gi-di! Si-gi-di!*", which meant that although there were only a hundred of them, they were equal to a thousand warriors.

Shaka became the hero of the Mthethwa people, not only because of his great courage and skill as a warrior and leader, but also because he was the best composer of songs, the most agile dancer, and the wittiest teller of stories. He soon grew rich with the cattle that Dingiswayo gave him, and he continued to think of even better ways to overcome the Mthethwa's enemies.

One of his battle plans was to split his warriors into three groups: the greatest number of men were to be in the middle, with two smaller, semi-circular groups on each side – like the head of a buffalo with two curved horns.

"Most of you warriors will fight in the centre!" he instructed his men. "The men on either side – the great horns – will surround the enemy and take them by surprise."

It was a brilliant idea. Dingiswayo was so impressed with Shaka's achievements that when Buza, the old commander of the Mthethwa army, retired, he announced that Shaka was to be the new commander.

Shaka proved to be a ruthless leader. He spared no lives if the enemy would not surrender, but with his own warriors he was generous and he always shared his prize of cattle amongst them. He made sure that all the wounded amongst his men received immediate attention, and were treated with medicines made by the doctors. Some of the medicines were made from the boiled intestines of oxen, and others from herbs, while wounds were dressed with soothing poultices made of crushed leaves.

Although Dingiswayo was pleased with Shaka's achievements, there were still certain matters upon which they disagreed.

"You are far too eager to destroy all our enemies, Shaka," he told him one night as they sat talking about their victories. "It is not always necessary to murder these men. We must simply teach them a lesson they will never forget."

"I cannot agree with you, Dingiswayo!" Shaka replied angrily, his eyes flashing in the darkness of the hut. "If we do not destroy these dogs, they will rise up and fight us again and again!"

Dingiswayo looked at Shaka and laughed. "You are indeed a brave warrior," he said, "but you still have a lot to learn."

Shaka glared at his chief, biting back the sharp words which were forming in his mouth. But what Dingiswayo said next made him tremble with pride and excitement.

"Shaka, when your father, Senzangakhona, dies, you will be chief of all the Zulu."

And so it was.

Shaka's regiments

When Shaka became chief of the Zulu clan he found, to his dismay, that his army consisted of only about 350 men – a sad little band of poorly trained soldiers. He started by dividing them into four distinct regiments, according to age. The youngest, called the Fasimba, *were trained in his own special way and they became his favourites.*

Shaka drilled his army with furious energy. At last he was able to put into practice all the tactics he had worked out during the years in Dingiswayo's army. Each regiment had its own battle cry, war songs and uniform of feathers and furs. Of course they all had to go barefooted, and learn how to use his special stabbing spear. Armed with Shaka's new, larger shields, he sent them out on endless exhausting marches, making them run up and down the hills and valleys until they were ready to drop. The discipline was so tight, and the training so strict, that from the very beginning they scored victories over the surrounding clans, and the numbers in his army increased rapidly as the defeated warriors joined his regiments.

When it came to controlling his army, Shaka saw to it

that a soldier who behaved in a cowardly way was punished or put to death, and one who showed courage in battle was richly rewarded. In this way his soldiers became fearless and obedient. Outstanding warriors were given one brilliant red feather from a lourie; but the greatest award for bravery was a necklace of olive wood. Each piece was carved so well that, when threaded on a cord, it fitted neatly with the next like the vertebrae in a backbone. The longer the necklace, the greater the honour.

Shaka's military disciplines succeeded brilliantly. By the time he died, his army had grown from a few hundred rough soldiers to 50 000 invincible warriors.

A new chief for the Zulu

It was a triumphant day for Shaka when, at the head of his bodyguard, and dressed in full battle dress, he strode into his father's kraal. Senzangakhona was dead, and Shaka was king of the Zulu. It was the same kraal from which he and Nandi had fled when he was a small, unhappy boy. How different the circumstances were now!

This was one of the proudest moments of his life. He walked slowly and with great dignity, his handsome face solemn, his piercing gaze sweeping proudly over the assembled people. Round his head he wore a circle of otter skin pierced with fiery red feathers, with a single blue crane feather in the middle. From his waist hung a kilt made of strips of fur rolled up to look like tails. Ox tails encircled his upper arms and his mighty calves, and over his shoulders and chest he wore a fringe of blue-grey monkey fur. In his left hand Shaka carried a snow-white shield with a single black spot; in the other; his famous stabbing spear.

The Zulu people gazed at him in fear and admiration. Then the hills echoed with the roar of the royal salute, "*Bayete, Nkosi! Bayete, Nkosi!* Hail, our king!"

"We shall have a great feast!" he roared in reply. "Kill the fattest oxen and bring the beer! The Great Elephant has arrived!"

Even as they celebrated, Shaka was making plans. First, he decided to build a new kraal. The place he chose for his new capital was on the banks of a wide stream. Bulawayo, the Place of Killing, was completed in a month, and consisted of one hundred huts. Twenty of these were for Shaka's use, for his mother Nandi, and his favourite woman, Pampata. Then he set about training his new Zulu army.

When he first saw them, he shook his head in disgust. "What am I to do," he thought, "with a little nest of scurrying ants in a territory so small that a man with strong legs can cross it in the time it takes the sun to rise?" But Shaka was not daunted by anything.

First, he provided the soldiers with short, stabbing spears like his own. Then he told them to take off their clumsy sandals and bury them.

There was much complaining among the older men about this new rule. "But how are we to run on the stony ground without sandals?"

"Are your feet so dainty that you fear a little thorn?" Shaka roared. Immediately he ordered that the parade ground be littered with small, sharp devil thorns, called *nKunzana*. "Now take off your clumsy sandals and crush every one of those thorns into the ground!" he bellowed.

Shaka himself led the wild dance of thorns. Any soldier who showed signs of pain or fear was clubbed to death.

"I will make brave warriors of you yet!" he shouted. When all the thorns had been stamped into the ground, he rewarded the men who had passed the test with beer and roast oxen.

Soon his army was ready for testing, but before setting out to conquer the surrounding clans, Shaka decided the time had come to take revenge on all those who had been unkind to him and Nandi.

"Now these people will pay for their evil words and deeds," he thought with satisfaction. "I, Shaka, will teach my people a lesson they will never forget."

Seating himself under a large tree at the top of the kraal, he called the culprits forward to be judged. He was ruthless, sparing no person who had ever offended him or his beloved Nandi. Scores of people were stabbed and clubbed to death, and the dust was stained red with blood. It was a grim day, and the Zulu realized that their new king was no weakling.

"*Indoda!*" they muttered as they returned to their huts, shaking with fear and relieved to be alive. "Our king is indeed a man to respect! He is truly a Great Elephant!"

Pampata

Although Shaka never married, he was extremely fond of a woman named Pampata, who was not only beautiful but intelligent and loving as well. From the start she prophesied that he would one day rule over an enormous kingdom. When he was away on the battlefield, Pampata bought charms from the medicine men to ensure his safe return. The Zulu believed that while a warrior was away fighting, his sleeping mat should rest against the wall at the back of the hut. If the mat fell down, it meant that its owner would die. So Pampata simply pegged Shaka's mat to the wall so that it could never fall. She was also fiercely loyal and always informed him of what his people were saying about him. Despite their love for each other, Shaka would not make her his bride.

"A man's sons can rise up against him," he said, "and for this reason I do not want any children."

Revenge against the enemy clans

Late one afternoon, Shaka summoned his warriors. "The time has come to attack the Langeni clan," he told his men. "We will march overnight and surround the kraal. When the sun rises, Chief Makedama will rub his eyes and howl in fright like a jackal in a trap."

And sure enough, the surprised Langeni chief surrendered without any fighting.

Shaka was overjoyed at his victory. He had never forgotten the unhappiness of his boyhood days amongst the Langeni, and he again ordered a trial of all those people who had been unkind to him and his mother.

"Take them away!" he commanded his guards, "and deal with these dogs as they deserve. Twist off their necks like chickens."

Having tasted victory, Shaka's craving for power grew ever stronger. He spent more and more of his time devising ways to increase the strength and size of his army. The fame of his regiments had spread far and wide, and soon soldiers from other clans were begging to be allowed to join.

Leading his army himself, and using the clever head, chest and horn formation, he completely overpowered his old enemies, the Buthelezi. One of the few to escape was their chief, Pungashe, who fled to Chief Zwide of the Ndwandwe clan for protection.

"This Shaka is a giant," he told Zwide, alarmed. "He knows no fear and his soldiers run faster than the wind. The ground shakes when they stamp their feet and the sky trembles with their war-cry!"

Zwide looked thoughtful. "Is that so?" he mused. "Well, we shall see who is the greatest power in this land. I, Zwide, am not afraid of a little beetle."

Before long the battle took place, and the two armies met at a nearby hill. The Ndwandwe army had about twice as many men as Shaka's army, but they knew nothing of his clever way of fighting.

"You will stay out of sight at the bottom of the hill," Shaka told his best regiments, "and the others will parade at the top, except for a few men who will drive off a herd of cattle."

It was a very shrewd plan. Many of the Ndwandwe chased after their cattle, while those who climbed to the top of the hill were met by wave after wave of Zulu warriors, who stormed up from the bottom. Several of Zwide's sons were killed, and finally the exhausted Ndwandwe withdrew.

Shaka knew that they would be back before long. "There are more Ndwandwe than Zulu warriors," he thought, "so I shall have to lead them into a trap."

First, he ordered his people to store all their grain in bags and hide these inside deep caves. Then he sent all the women and children to hide in the forest, telling them to take the cattle with them.

When Zwide's men came back to revenge their defeat, they found the valley deserted. Where were the Zulu? There was not a person to be seen anywhere. No grain lay on the land, and no cattle moved in the kraals. It was silent, empty country.

The Ndwandwe leader and his thousands of men were very confused. What were they to eat when their scant food supplies ran out? And where was the Zulu army? He scented trouble, and decided to camp for the night in a nearby forest while he thought about what to do next.

Meanwhile, not far away, Shaka and his warriors

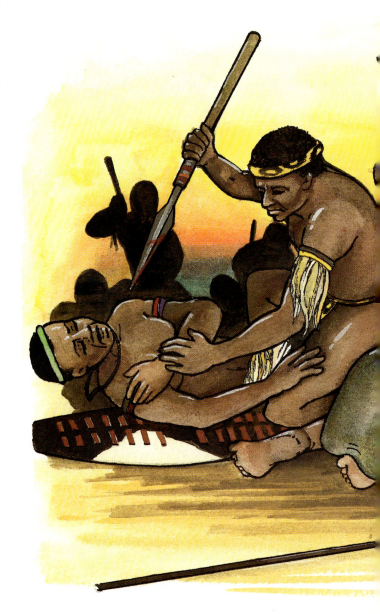

were also camping out, feasting off roasted meat and waiting for the order to advance.

Shaka called up five hundred men. "You are to steal into the middle of those sleeping Ndwandwe weasels," he said. "It is dark, our uniform is similar, and our language is the same. If they question you, tell them you are Ndwandwe returning from a scouting party. Crawl into their midst, lie down like shadows amongst them, and when your leader gives the signal, you stab them as they lie."

The result was chaotic. The Ndwandwe warriors woke up to find themselves being attacked by hun-dreds of shadowy figures, the polished metal of their sharp spears flashing in the moonlight.

"Witchcraft is at work!" they screamed, fleeing in terror. "Who are these wizards who rise up in our midst and attack us?"

Shaka's army set out in pursuit. The battle raged for days and eventually reached a climax at the Mhlatuze River, where many of the Ndwandwe warriors were killed. Outnumbered and its power broken, Zwide's army fled.

Soon Shaka was hailed as one of the most powerful leaders ever known.

The harvest festival

One hot day in summer Shaka called all of his people together.

"It is time to hold a harvest festival, a great *Mkosi*," he announced.

Amongst the Zulu, harvest time was always a period of rejoicing and great celebration. Each December, when the fruit and vegetables ripened and were ready for eating, a festival was held. They always waited for the full moon before holding the festival, and no-one was allowed to eat any of the newly-ripened crops until after the celebrations. It was also a time for strengthening the king and his army with special medicines, and for making new laws.

"We must not forget," Shaka continued, "to make sacrifices to the spirits of our forefathers and give thanks for their help and protection."

Thousands of people flocked to the royal kraal in great excitement. All the warriors arrived wearing their full battle-dress, bringing their fattest cattle to slaughter for the feast. Before any feasting could begin, however, an important ritual had to take place – Killing the Bull. This bull had to be stolen overnight from one of the enemy tribes.

"Choose the fiercest black beast you can find," Shaka commanded, "and let my youngest regiment throw him to the ground and strangle him with their bare hands. Then we shall roast his flesh and eat it for medicine."

For one night and two days Shaka stayed inside his royal hut, while his doctors fussed around him, painting his face and body with coloured powders and offering him their special mixtures of roots and plants, parts of the black bull and the fats of wild animals. At sunset on the second day, dressed in skins and decorated with maize leaves, beads and bangles, Shaka came out of the hut to spit out the medicine – first at the setting sun, and later into a roaring fire.

"U! U!" his people chanted. "See how our king spits out the evil and destroys the wicked spirits! U! U! Now we will be safe from the wizards!"

After his warriors had been given special strips of ox meat to eat, and had bathed in the river, the feasting and dancing began. It was a magnificent sight! Proudly Shaka stood on top of a high clay mound on the edge of the parade ground. On his right, on a pile of rush mats, sat Nandi, and next to her was seated his sister Nomcoba, who had grown into a beautiful young girl.

Before them swirled a surging sea of stamping, chanting warriors, ostrich plumes waving, white and black shields making patterns as their lines wove in and out, with the beads and bracelets worn by Shaka's regiment of young maidens flashing and sparkling a

they caught the sun. And when Shaka stepped into their midst and led the singing, the whole world seemed to shiver and shake.

At a harvest festival it was the custom that anyone could criticize the king, or ask him cheeky questions, without being put to death.

A soldier stepped out from the crowd. "When, oh Great Elephant, will we warriors be allowed to marry?" he asked boldly, for Shaka had forbidden them to take wives.

"When a soldier has reached a mature age and proved himself in battle," came the reply. "A married man does not make a good warrior. As you know, I set the example. I have not taken a wife, and I have no children."

"*Bayete!*" the crowd roared. "This is the truth!"

The next man stepped forward. "You say you do not wish to have children because they might threaten your power. But why do you allow your half-brother Dingane to walk like a shadow around you?"

Dingane was the son of Senzangakhona's sixth wife, and his ambition was to succeed his father as chief of the Zulu clan.

There was a sudden hush as the people gazed in fear at the man, astounded at his courage in asking the king such a question. Shaka would surely have him put to death for his impertinence! The warriors held their breath as their king considered the question in silence.

"Must I kill my father's son?" asked Shaka at last.

The questioner shook his head anxiously. "But beware, my king," he said in a trembling voice. "He looks at you with evil eyes."

Shaka shook his head, unconcerned, and beckoned the next questioner. Little did he know that he should have paid attention to these solemn words of warning.

The growing of crops

The growing of crops was the job of the Zulu women. Mothers and their daughters worked in the gardens with their hoes every day, planting and weeding the pumpkins and beans, groundnuts and maize. The small boys in each family were sent to the fields before dawn to shout at the birds and keep them away from the crops by continual stone-throwing, while at night it became the duty of men to guard the gardens against porcupines and other night animals. They held all sorts of beliefs about how to ensure a good harvest.

"To make the grain grow tall," mothers would advise their daughters, "you must never point at a vegetable with your finger, or carry a fowl through a field of ripening maize, or it will all wither and die."

The great hunt

After years of fighting battles and conquering his enemies, Shaka decided it was time for some relaxation.

"We will have a hunt," he announced. "A great royal hunt such as has never been seen before!" He sent for a team of young boys to deliver the message throughout the territory. "Tell all the men to smear their bodies with fat to make them fast and strong," he commanded. "And let them sharpen their hunting spears, collect their clubs, their axes and their shields, and come at once to Bulawayo."

Shaka organized his great hunt as carefully as he planned his battles. The area he chose lay between two rivers.

"You will dig deep pits," he instructed his men. "Cover these pits with branches and grass, and on either side you will build fences out of thorn trees.

His plan was that lines of men would drive the wild animals towards the spot where the rivers joined. The animals which did not fall into the pits would be speared by hunters waiting behind the fences, while those which managed to get through would be trapped in the wedge where the two rivers met.

It was at dawn on a calm spring morning when Shaka and his hunters took up their positions on a high ridge. In the valley below, other men waded through the long grass, shouting and beating the ground with sticks in order to drive the animals towards the royal party.

Shaka became very excited when he saw the first puffs of dust in the still morning air. "Hah!" he roared. "The elephants are coming! See how they kick up the earth! They are afraid, for they know the greatest elephant of all is waiting for them!"

Minutes later the first herd was upon them, trumpeting in fury as it thundered up the hill. Shaka waited until an enormous young bull elephant passed by, and then with a wild cry he attacked its hind legs with his razor-sharp axe, cutting right through the tendons of its heels. The bull sank to his knees with a bellow of rage. Another elephant, in front, sensed danger, and he turned around, spread his enormous ears and with a terrifying shriek charged straight towards Shaka.

"Quick," screamed two of the hunters. "Our king will be crushed like an ant!" And without a thought for their own safety, they jumped into the path of the raging beast. Grabbing one of the men with his trunk, the elephant hurled him to his death, while the other was trampled under his mighty foot. This gave Shaka time to jump out of his path. Without wasting a second, he picked himself up and sprang forward to slash the hind legs of the elephant.

Later, he rewarded the dead men's families with several head of cattle. The tusks of the elephant he kept for himself, for they were a royal prize.

No sooner had the agonized cries of many wounded elephants died on the morning air than Shaka became aware of a different sound. Like a roaring wind, a huge rhinoceros rushed up the slope, brushing right past the fence behind which Shaka stood. In a flash, Shaka leapt through a gap in the fence, lunged out and sank his axe into one of the rhino's back legs. Like a mighty, snorting steam engine, the furious beast turned round and thundered back down the slope. Shaka stood right in its path. For a split second he was too stunned to move, and then, like a bolt of lightning, he leapt up and flung himself out of the path of the charging rhinocerous.

"Be careful, my king!" shouted Mgobozi. "You will be torn to pieces if you do not move to a safer place!"

But Shaka was enjoying himself immensely, and he turned to Mgobozi and scoffed, "Do you think your king is like *iJikijolo*, a soft little berry that can be squashed between the fingers of a child?" Annoyed by Mgobozi's warning, he stamped his foot on the hard ground. The movement almost caused his death, because it attracted the attention of a huge buffalo. Churning round, it plunged its whole head through the fence, and suddenly Shaka found a pair of massive horns on a level with his face. This time he stood frozen with shock, but the faithful Mgobozi jumped forward and waved his club above his head to distract the buffalo. Several other men dived forward and finished off the fierce beast with their clubs. The steady thumping of the beaters' sticks on the grass set up a wild stampede of other animals: wildebeest and giraffe, zebra and wild pig, jackal and hyena and a magnificent, powerful leopard.

"*Dadwetu!*" exclaimed Mgobozi, exhausted. "Has the Great Elephant not had enough?"

But Shaka was waiting for the king of the beasts. "We shall see who is the greater king!" he cried, his voice echoing out across the hills. It was only after they had driven three whole prides of lions between the fences and finished them off with their strong spears in a terrible, gory battle, that he allowed his weary men to retire.

There was no time to rest, however, for all the meat now had to be cut up and dried over a fire. All night they slaughtered and feasted on the livers and hearts of the animals and the next day, carrying tusks and skins and great loads of game, Shaka and his hunters marched triumphantly back to Bulawayo.

The new Bulawayo

Shaka's kingdom had become so vast that he decided it was time he built a new royal kraal.

"This old kraal is too small for me," he mused. "I must build a big, new capital in a more central position. A kraal that is truly fitting for a king as mighty and powerful as I am."

The site he chose was on a ridge above a deep valley. The new Bulawayo was enormous, with Shaka's big royal hut situated at the head of a circle of thousands of other huts, with a large cattle kraal in the middle. Not far away he built a smaller kraal especially for Nandi. From Bulawayo Shaka ruled his mighty kingdom.

Early every morning, just after the sun rose, Shaka's Court of Justice was held. For anybody who had displeased him, this was a terrifying ordeal. Splendidly dressed in his warrior clothes, Shaka took his place on the royal throne, which consisted of a bundle of rolled-up mats under a giant fig tree. On one side stood his councillors and on the other a group of executioners holding heavy clubs, while the court praisers set up a loud chorus.

"Here sits our king! See the Great Elephant who crushes his enemies, the mighty bull whose voice shakes the heavens, the lion of all lions who eats the sun and spits fire at the moon! Here sits Shaka, before whose might all men crawl in the dust. *Bayete!*"

One by one his quaking subjects appeared. One of them had trespassed on another's grazing ground, one had stolen another man's wife, and another had proved cowardly in battle. In a chillingly soft voice Shaka questioned them, listening intently to their answers, occasionally frowning and seldom taking his piercing eyes off the trembling man's face. He did not take long to reach his decision.

If the verdict was guilty, he uttered the dreaded command, "Take him away! I have spoken!" To be 'taken away' meant death.

"*Bayete!*" the condemned men murmured meekly as they were led away. "The king's will shall be done!"

At about ten o'clock the court was adjourned so that Shaka could have his daily bath. As usual, this was taken in front of all the people, and was a social and merry occasion.

"We Zulu like a person to smell of water," he remarked, accepting gourds filled with water from his attendants. After he had rinsed his body, Shaka was given a wooden dish containing a paste of fat and ground millet. Scooping up handfuls of this soapy mixture, he rubbed himself all over and then rinsed it

away with fresh water. Then he reached for his cosmetics, red ochre paste and butter, which he rubbed into his huge body until it shone.

After he had tied on his fur kilt, he sat down to his morning meal – a feast of maize porridge sweetened with honey, bowls of cooked spinach and strips of grilled meat which he ate with his fingers, all washed down with a calabash of sour milk. After the meal, the court started up again and continued until the middle of the afternoon, after which Shaka and his councillors retired to the coolness of the great council hut to discuss other important affairs. One of these matters concerned the Pepeta clan, who lived like dassies at the very top of a mountain.

Mgobozi: A faithful friend

Mgobozi was certainly Shaka's closest friend. From the time they were both young boys, Mgobozi was his follower and protector, and he later became his leading warrior.

Because of his bravery in battle, Shaka gave Mgobozi special permission to marry. When Mgobozi chose twenty brides at the same time, Shaka was highly amused and gave him a generous present of several goats and head of cattle. He also instructed a special guard to stay close to him in battle, for Mgobozi was inclined to get very excited and to take terrible risks. It was Mgobozi who had saved Shaka's life on the Great Hunt. Later he again risked his life, this time by insulting his chief because he was worried about Shaka's safety.

"You are stupid and childish because you have always refused a bodyguard!" he burst out. "You have many enemies and will surely be killed by one of them! And now you may kill me – for I have dared to question the wisdom of the Great Elephant!"

"Mgobozi," replied Shaka gravely, "I would sooner die than harm you, for we are as one person."

In the end it was Mgobozi's fearlessness which caused his death. In a battle against their old enemies, the Ndwandwe, he rushed in and tore right through the warriors, only to find that he was hopelessly outnumbered and cut off from the rest of his army. Eventually he collapsed from stab wounds, and died. It is said that Shaka personally went to the battlefield to search for the body of his friend, and that he wept when he found it.

Shaka's millipede

Shaka's experiences in battle had taught him that he always had to be on the alert and ready for attack.

"That is the only way I will keep my power and control my empire," he told himself.

One day he heard that there was a great deal of fighting and bloodshed in the south. He summoned several hundred of his warriors immediately.

"We will march at once," he commanded. After travelling for some days, Shaka and his army found themselves at the foot of a very strange mountain. It was steep and fairly high, and had a flat top surrounded on all sides by towering cliffs.

This was where Chief Mshika of the Pepeta clan lived. He had decided to settle on top of the mountain because it was a natural fortress. The only way a person could reach the top was by climbing a long ladder, which was let down only when Mshika's subjects needed to carry up baskets of food. Drinking water was available from nearby springs, and so the clan managed to live very comfortably in their unusual stronghold.

Shaka studied the mountain in silence for a few minutes, then he turned to his chief warrior and best friend, Mgobozi.

"Mgobozi," he said, "are these eyes of mine bewitched? Do you see dassies and baboons on the top of that mountain? Or do you, like me, see hundreds of people?"

Mgobozi gazed earnestly skywards. "People, my king? Living on that little antheap? It is not possible!" But even as he looked, his smile faded and his eyebrows sprang together into a frown. He could see men ducking behind rocks and ridges, spying on them. Some of them were picking up stones and rocks to throw down on the Zulu warriors below.

"*Nkosi!*" exlaimed Mgobozi, dodging a stone from above, "let us leave this place before these baboons find their aim!"

"Leave?" demanded Shaka. "Am I to be frightened by this nest of little ants?" He had noticed that there was a way of getting up one of the cliffs, and was already working out a plan of attack. First, he commanded that several oxen be killed, and their hides cut into long strips. These strips were tied together to make ropes, and a stone was tied to the end of each. Then he ordered some of his warriors to throw the ropes over the branches of high trees, while others had to practise climbing up the thongs, with their shields and spears tied to their backs.

Mgobozi shook his head in disbelief. "What is it you are doing, my chief? Why do you ask your warriors to climb the trees like monkeys?"

Shaka grinned at Mgobozi. "Just wait and see." He knew exactly what he was doing. After a while, he summoned the warriors who were the best climbers.

"You will form a *songololo*, a little millipede!" he roared. "A column of men, standing five deep. Those warriors on the outside must walk with their shields at their sides, those at the front of the column with their shields in front of them, and those in the middle with their shields over their heads. Your shields must overlap like the scales of a fish!" Shaka's exhausted warriors looked at each other in surprise, but they did not dare argue.

Long before the sun rose the next morning, this strange, shuffling *songololo* slowly inched its way up a steep gully in the mountain. Ahead of it sped several agile young boys, who looped the leather ropes over the bushes that were growing in cracks in the rock. Slowly the *songololo* pulled itself up the mountain. Meanwhile, Shaka and the other warriors distracted the Pepeta by storming around to the other side of the mountain and hurling their spears into the air. When the millipede had nearly reached the top it was noticed by some Pepeta women who were looking over the edge. They rushed screaming to their chief.

"A great scaly creature is crawling up our mountain!" they shrieked.

"We must stop this thing with stones and spears!" their chief cried. "We cannot allow this monster to climb any higher!"

But Shaka's warriors were protected by their shields. The millipede reached the top and simply went right on marching through the Pepeta people, who fled in all directions, screaming in terror. A few of them tried to climb down the ladder, but the rest were trapped on top of the mountain. Most were stabbed by Shaka's warriors, while some jumped over the edge and died on the rocks far below.

And so Shaka added yet another gory battle to his list of victories. Only Pampata was not impressed, for she worried about his terrible hunger for power.

"If a tree grows too proud and spreads its branches too wide," she warned, "they will grow weak and break off."

But Shaka had no intention of heeding her advice. A great king such as he had too many enemies, and he knew he could not afford to relax.

Mzilikazi's treachery

One friend of Shaka's who later became his enemy, was Mzilikazi, a chief of the Khumalo clan. Because he was aware of Shaka's great power, Mzilikazi asked if he could join his army, and promised him his loyalty and support. He was an excellent soldier and soon became one of Shaka's favourites. When Shaka decided to attack a clan in the north, he called Mzilikazi to the royal hut.

"I have chosen you to be commander of the expedition," he said, handing him a splendid battle-dress and a large white shield. "Go safely, my friend, and after the battle you may once again live as chief of your Khumalo clan."

Mzilikazi won the battle, but he did not return to Bulawayo and he did not send any of the captured cattle back to Shaka. Shaka was surprised and angry,

and sent some messengers to demand the cattle. Mzilikazi replied by defiantly cutting off the plumes on the messengers' headdresses.

"Let the old elephant fetch them himself!" he declared. Shaka then sent a regiment to fetch Mzilikazi, but the Khumalo warriors were ready for them. They gathered on the slopes of a mountain and pushed boulders and rocks down on to the approaching Zulu army.

"Is this the friend to whom I gave so much?" Shaka asked sorrowfully, and he sent out another regiment.

After a bloody battle, Mzilikazi trekked northwards and settled in what is today known as Zimbabwe. Like Shaka, he called his capital Bulawayo. Shaka never forgot Mzilikazi's treachery, for he had regarded the young man as a son.

Witchcraft at Bulawayo

Witchcraft was a powerful force in the life of the Zulu. They believed that witches and wizards used their magical powers and their dreadful medicines – made from pieces of the human body and the tails and eyebrows of baboons – to cause all sorts of misfortunes.

If a man suddenly fell ill, he thought it was because he had been bewitched. If a woman was unable to have children, she blamed the wizards. So every kraal employed several diviners, or *sangomas*, whose job it was to expose or 'smell out' these evil people, so that they could be punished.

Shaka respected these *sangomas* and recognized their power and influence over his people. But he also suspected that some of them were cheats, who 'smelt out' certain people because they happened to dislike them. One of these *sangomas* was an old woman called Nobela. She had once made the mistake of trying to 'smell out' Shaka's friend Mgobozi, simply because he had spat when her name was mentioned. So Shaka decided to teach Nobela – and all the other *sangomas* – a lesson.

One night, when everyone was asleep, Shaka asked one of his servants, Mbopa, to bring him a pot filled with blood, and a brush made from the tail of an ox. Stealthily he crept outside and, dipping the tail into the pot, he spattered the walls of his royal hut with the blood, and shook blobs of it all over the ground. Then he gave the brush and the pot back to Mbopa, and went to sleep.

When the sun rose the next morning and the people saw the blood smears, they shuddered in fear.

"Who has dared to do such an evil thing?" they asked each other, wailing and stamping the earth in terror. "Witchcraft is surely at work!"

Rubbing his eyes, Shaka came out of his hut. He took one look at the blood and, slamming one fist into the other he thundered, "*Dadwetu!* I see before me the work of a wizard! These are the signs of an evil snake that slithers in the night!"

The people shook their heads in dismay. "This is indeed the work of wizards," they agreed.

"Send for the *sangomas*!" Shaka roared. "Let them find the wizard who has done this wicked deed! I, Shaka, will have a smelling out as never before!"

Early the next morning, thousands of people gathered in the cattle-kraal for the 'smelling out' parade. When the sun rose, there was not a sound to be heard, for everyone sat silent and afraid, thinking, "If they choose me, I shall have to die."

Suddenly the air trembled with a ghastly wailing and moaning, and through a side gate crept a hideous, screeching, snaking line of *sangomas*, crouching and sniffing the ground and then leaping into the air. At the head of the line was Nobela, wrapped in the skin of a python with its wide-open jaws propped on top of her head. Wound around her legs were the intestines of a cow, stuffed with fat and blood, and her clay-smeared body was decorated with human teeth, medicine bags, and bunches of roots and bones. In one hand she held the tail of a wildebeest, which she used for 'smelling out' the wizards. Once she had chosen a culprit, she would hit him over the head with this tail. This was a sign that he should be led away and have his skull crushed.

With a wild shriek, Nobela leapt upon Mbopa, the man who had brought Shaka the pot of ox blood, and hit him over the head.

"That was your first mistake," thought Shaka grimly, but he said nothing. Then Nobela walked slowly towards Shaka's half-brothers, Dingane and Mhlangana, her eyes glittering.

"Leave my father's sons alone, you old woman!" bellowed Shaka.

She turned to him, and shrieked, "Very well, my king! But you would do well to heed my warning!"

The 'smelling out' carried on all afternoon, and the wildebeest tails came down on many innocent heads. Shaka watched the proceedings with great interest, wondering if the *sangomas* would discover the truth. Suddenly he noticed that there were only two *sangomas* who had not smelt anybody out. All day they had sat quietly to one side, deep in thought. He beckoned to them, and they walked slowly up to him.

One of them took a deep breath. "It is Shaka who spattered the blood in the night!" he announced.

"Yes, it was the king! Shaka, and no other!" said the other *sangoma*. The crowd gasped in disbelief. These men would surely be put to death for accusing Shaka of witchcraft!

With a triumphant shout Shaka rose from the royal throne. "Of all the *sangomas* you are the only two who have spoken the truth!" he roared. "Yes, I, Shaka, did the deed! It was I who smeared blood on the walls of the hut!" There was a stunned silence.

Shaka pointed at the *sangomas*, who stood huddled together in terror. "At last I have proved that all but two of you are liars and cheats! You accused every man but me of this wicked deed!" Then he turned to the crowd. "What are we to do with these cowards?" he demanded.

"They must be killed!" screamed his people, surging forward. "Put them to death immediately, *Nkosi!*"

In the confusion that followed, nobody saw Nobela slip away. When her turn came to be executed, she was found sitting quite still against a pole with an empty gourd in her hand. Nobela had swallowed poison, and was dead.

Shaka and the British

During the year 1824, two sailing ships billowed into the bay at Port Natal. The first to arrive was the *Julia*, carrying twenty-six passengers, one of whom was an adventurous young man by the name of Henry Francis Fynn. The *Antelope* arrived two months later, with Lieutenant George Francis Farewell in command. These men wanted to start a trading station in Natal, and barter their goods for ivory, rhinoceros horns and hippopotamus teeth. Fynn and Farewell had heard a great deal about Shaka and his achievements, and they knew they would need to discuss their plans with him first. So messengers were sent to Bulawayo to ask for permission to visit the king.

When he heard the messenger's request, Shaka called his advisers together. "I have had news," he told them, "of some very strange visitors." His advisers exchanged surprised glances. "It is said that these men have skin the colour of milk and eyes as blue as the feathers of a crane."

"This cannot be true!" they exclaimed.

"It is my plan," he continued, "to welcome these people, for I have heard that their knowledge is great. I wish to see them with my own eyes and hear what they have to say to me."

Eagerly, his advisers nodded in agreement. "But!" and Shaka held up his hand. "They shall come to Bulawayo only when the Great Elephant is ready for them!" Shaka was determined to impress his visitors, and he wanted time to organize a display of his might.

In due course a messenger was sent to fetch Fynn and Farewell. Thirteen days later they galloped into the great kraal. A roar of surprise went up from the mass of Zulu who had gathered to greet them. Towering over his people like a giant tree in a young forest, Shaka invited the men to sit in front of his throne.

"You have seen the vastness of my kingdom," he told them. "You have no doubt seen the big kraals, the thousands of huts and the fat cattle."

"Yes, *Nkosi*," responded the visitors politely. "Yes, we have seen how prosperous your kingdom is!"

Shaka nodded. "Soon I shall show you greater things," he went on, "but first you will tell me of your land and your king."

He listened carefully to what they told him, interrupting now and then with a question. "This King George of yours who lives in England, this *Joji*, does he have a big army?"

"Oh, yes," they replied. "A mighty army indeed."

"Then he must have many cattle. What does he do with the hides of his cattle?"

His visitors looked at each other. "Well, they are used to make shoes," one of them mumbled.

Shaka slapped his knee in glee. He was enjoying making fun of his visitors. "To make shoes? They are not used for shields? *Dadwetu*, but you white men must have very soft feet!" He was equally scornful of the clothes they wore, yet he was overjoyed with the splendid military coat they had brought him as a gift.

Early the next morning, Fynn and Farewell were invited to watch a parade. What a spectacle Shaka had organized for his guests! A sea of warriors in full battle-dress rattled their shields and pounded the earth with their bare feet, while wave after wave of cattle thundered past, each herd in a different colour. Regiments of gaily decorated dancing girls swayed gracefully and sang songs praising Shaka.

Several times Shaka leapt up and joined in the dancing, until finally everyone was exhausted and ready for a feast.

After the celebrations had come to an end, Farewell returned to Port Natal. Fynn decided to stay on at Bulawayo for a while, and little did he know that he would help to save Shaka's life.

One dark, moonless night, Fynn was watching some dancers perform in the royal kraal. Suddenly he heard a terrible, anguished scream.

"Shaka has been stabbed!" somebody shouted. "The lion of lions roars and bleeds and lies on the ground!" The crowd became hysterical, sobbing and wailing and bumping into each other in the dark. Alarmed, Fynn hurried away to brew some herb tea, and then went to the hut where Shaka had been taken. He found the king lying groaning in agony on his mat. An assassin had thrust a spear through Shaka's left arm, and it had pierced his ribs. Carefully Fynn bathed and bandaged the wound, while Shaka's doctors plied him with medicines.

It was a dreadful night. Outside the hut, Shaka's subjects chanted and moaned in terrified grief. Many stumbled, or fainted and were trampled, and those who became too exhausted to weep any longer were immediately put to death.

When Farewell heard of the attack on Shaka's life, he returned to Bulawayo. To his relief, he found that the king had recovered, and he took the opportunity to persuade Shaka to grant him full possession of Port Natal and much of the land on either side. Triumphantly he rode back to start building a settlement, in the same place where Durban stands today.

This was not the last visit these men and other white traders paid to Shaka's kraal during their adventurous years in Natal. They visited him regularly, bringing him loads of the gifts they knew he loved – brass bars and beads and blankets. They knew that, in order to survive, they had to remain on good terms with the Zulu king who could be as cruel as he could be kind.

John Ross

John Ross was a remarkable young boy who made a great impression on Shaka.

He was only fifteen years old when, in 1825, he landed at Port Natal. The ship on which he had sailed had run aground at the entrance to the harbour, and all the medical supplies on board had been lost. The people of the settlement at Port Natal needed these medical supplies desperately, and Lieutenant King, their commander, decided to send Ross to Delagoa Bay to obtain them.

"This is a very dangerous mission," he told the boy, "but I have no choice but to send you. I cannot spare another man."

John set off immediately. Delagoa Bay lay about five hundred kilometres to the north, and the country through which he had to travel was unexplored and very dangerous. There were no paths or roads, and the dark, dense forests and surrounding veld still teemed with wild animals. The area was also inhabited by several hostile clans.

In spite of all these dangers, however, John and his two servants arrived safely at Bulawayo. Shaka was astonished, because no white man had completed this journey and lived to tell the tale.

"This boy surely has the heart of a lion!" Shaka exclaimed. He was so impressed by John's courage that he provided him with an escort of soldiers and a gift of some elephant tusks, which he could give to the Portuguese at Delagoa Bay in exchange for the necessary medicines.

At first the Portuguese thought Ross was a spy.

"Who would be so foolish to send such a young boy on such a dangerous journey just to fetch medical supplies?" they asked each other suspiciously.

Eventually John persuaded them that he was telling the truth. They accepted Shaka's ivory and gave the boy the supplies he needed.

He returned safely to Port Natal, knowing that if it had not been for Shaka's kindness, his journey might not have had such a happy ending.

The death of Nandi

Shaka had the greatest respect and a very deep affection for his mother. Ever since the day that he and Nandi had been driven away from Senzangakhona's kraal, he had been fiercely protective of her, determined that no-one would treat her unkindly again.

Years before, when he was still a herd-boy, he had said to his mother: "One day when I am king, you will be a great queen and share all my cattle."

"You make me very happy, my son" Nandi had responded with a smile. "And when I am a grandmother I shall care for your children with all the love in my heart."

Shaka had shaken his head stubbornly. "I shall never marry, Mother."

Little did Nandi know that Shaka would never change his mind. She could not understand his fear of having sons who might one day try to snatch his throne, and as she grew older she complained more often.

"Mother, you are like a fussy old hen," Shaka told her one day. "I am no longer a little chicken. Do not cluck over me!"

"If you are no longer a chicken, where are your sons?" Nandi snapped. "Where are my grandchildren? I am rich with cattle and I have my own kraal, but I am also getting old and I want a grandchild! I want a little bull calf to care for!" The tears rolled slowly down her withered cheeks.

Shaka sighed deeply and looked away from his mother. He hated to see her upset, but how could he make her understand that he did not want children?

Not long after this, one of Shaka's favourite women gave birth to a child, a boy who looked just like Shaka. Nandi was overjoyed, and keeping the birth a secret, she took the child to live with her at her kraal.

Shaka heard rumours about the boy, however, and one morning he decided to pay his mother a surprise visit. He found her playing with the baby in front of her hut.

"Whose child is this, Mother?" he asked.

Terrified that he would order the death of her grandson, Nandi replied in a shaking voice: "It is your child, my son. Can you not see the likeness?" She held him up. "See! He is smiling at you." She managed to persuade Shaka not to kill the child, but he insisted that the child and his mother be sent to another kraal far away.

Nandi missed the boy terribly. She had waited for a grandchild for so many years, and now he was gone.

She became more and more depressed, and not long afterwards she fell ill. Shaka was away hunting elephants, and a messenger was sent to tell him about his mother's illness. With a heavy heart, he hurried back to her kraal. It was too late. Nandi was unconscious, and she died a few hours later.

Shaka could not believe his mother was dead. He stood with his head resting on his shield, weeping. Then he broke out into a terrible shrieking and shouting. "Alas, my mother! My mother!"

This was the start of days and nights of hysterical grief. Mourners worked themselves up into a frenzy, weeping and wailing and clubbing each other to death, trying to prove their grief to their king. Those who stopped crying because they were too exhausted to carry on were executed.

No-one could comfort Shaka. His beloved mother was dead, and in his heart of hearts he knew that she had never forgiven him for sending her beloved grandson away.

After two days, a grave was dug for Nandi under the burial tree, and a special regiment of warriors was assigned to guard the grave for a whole year. During this period of mourning, no man was allowed to cultivate his land; no milk was drunk; and any woman who fell pregnant was put to death, together with her husband.

During this reign of terror, Shaka became deeply depressed, and lost all interest in governing his kingdom. "I have conquered the world," he cried, "but all the joy has gone out of my life!"

He decided that witches must have caused Nandi's death, and had several women burnt alive.

After three months, Shaka's kingdom was almost completely devastated. There was hardly any food for the people and, because they were forbidden to drink it, the precious milk from their cattle simply had to be poured onto the ground. Shaka's people grew angry about this wastage and some did not bother to hide their frustration. Faithful Pampata realized what was happening and tried to warn the melancholy king.

"Your people have suffered enough and are dying of starvation!" she told him. "You are destroying your country, and your nation will lose its respect for you."

Shaka stared at her with glazed eyes. He was so wrapped up in his own grief that he hardly heard her warning.

But Pampata spoke the truth. Shaka's reign – once so dazzling and powerful – had started its sad decline.

The Zulu and their cattle

Cattle were of the utmost importance to the Zulu. They provided meat and sour milk – staples of the Zulu diet – and a man's wealth was judged by the number of cattle he owned. It was the job of young boys to herd their fathers' cattle, while the older boys were chosen to watch the royal herds. The tasks of cooking, making beer and growing crops were left to the women.

The Zulu loved to ornament their favourite cattle by cutting their ears into strange shapes, or slitting and tying up the skins of their necks to look like buttons and tassels. Sometimes they even trained their horns to grow in different shapes and directions. Over the years they developed all sorts of medicines for curing cattle diseases, which were often made from the hair and skin of hyenas and from the fat of hippopotamuses.

Shaka was immensely proud of his cattle. He divided his herds into colours, with as many as five thousand in one herd: snow-white, pitch-black, ruddy red, or of mixed colours bred to a definite pattern.

In this way different coloured shields could be made. Two large shields could be made from one hide, and a skilled shield-maker could complete more than twenty a day. To make a shield, a hide was first pegged out on the ground to dry. Then it was scraped and dried and placed overnight under a layer of cow dung, and after that it was ready for cutting up. The hides of bulls were preferred because these made the strongest shields. Shaka allowed very few red shields to be made. He preferred black and white shields, and the more experienced a warrior, the whiter his shield was.

The last days of Shaka

After the death of Nandi, Shaka became increasingly moody and bad-tempered.

"I am growing old, I have lost my mother and my best friend, and now I feel the power slipping through these fingers," he muttered, staring at his hands.

The year before Nandi had died, he had built a new capital, Dukuza, close to Port Natal. It was here that he sat on a rock overlooking his kraal, brooding for hours about the problems of shaping his people into an even mightier nation. He seemed to sense, however, that he no longer had their full support, and at the back of his mind there loomed the shadowy threat of an unknown enemy.

Although Shaka did not know it, his most dangerous enemies were members of his close family circle – his aunt, Mkhabayi, his half-brothers Dingane and Mhlangana, and his servant Mbopa. Little did he suspect what an evil plot they were hatching.

To announce the end of the period of mourning for Nandi, Shaka decided to stage a military expedition against the Pondo people in the south.

"We shall wipe out all those who did not mourn for my mother," he announced. With terrifying swiftness, his warriors swept across the country, looting and killing and burning kraals.

But this dreadful campaign did not quench Shaka's thirst for power. He was still not satisfied, and so he sent them on another military expedition, against the Soshangane in the north. Dingane and Mhlangana, his half-brothers, were included in one of the regiments. As they were leaving, Mkhabayi, Shaka's aunt, beckoned them into her hut.

"Shaka will destroy us all in his terrible craving for power!" she hissed. "It is not only the blood of his enemies he lusts after! He wants the blood of his own people too! The time has come for action!"

"What is it you want us to do, Mkhabayi?" asked Dingane.

"You must kill the king!" she whispered. "Before his madness destroys us all."

The brothers set out with the rest of their regiment, but before they had got very far away from the kraal, they approached their commander.

"We are ill," they lied, "and sick soldiers are no good for fighting. We must return to Dukuza."

Minutes later, they were on their way back to the kraal. After a secret meeting with Mbopa, Shaka's servant, they were ready to put their murderous plan into operation.

Late that afternoon, Shaka went to receive a party of Bechuana people, who had come with gifts of feathers and animal skins. He was angry because he had expected them much earlier in the day.

"Why are you so late?" he thundered.

Mbopa was standing nearby, and he saw his chance. Pretending to be angry, he shouted, "Why did you keep the king waiting?" and rushed at them with a stout stick.

Dingane and Mhlangana were waiting behind the kraal fence with their spears concealed beneath their cloaks. They sprang forward and pounced on Shaka, who whirled round in surprise.

"You shall never see the sun set again," screamed Dingane, while Mhlangana drove his spear through the king's arm.

"What is the matter, my father's children? Why are you doing this to me?" gasped Shaka in shocked disbelief as both Dingane and Mbopa followed up the attack, plunging their spears into his body again and again. Then he crumpled, and fell to the ground. The Great Elephant was dead.

A deathly hush fell over the kraal as the crowd stared numbly at the body of their king, lying in a pool of blood. They could not believe that Shaka was dead. Seconds later, the valleys reverberated with the shrieking and wailing of thousands of anguished voices.

"The mountain has collapsed!" they cried. "The king is dead!"

Shaka was buried the next day, his body wrapped in a black ox skin. His personal possessions – royal clothes, weapons, beads and food pots – were all placed in the grave with him. A stone lid and thorn bushes were used to cover the grave, for the Zulu people believed that his spirit might escape, and take revenge on his murderers.

Without Shaka, the mighty Zulu nation gradually declined in power and glory. He was their great warrior and their shining hero, alternately loved and feared, hated and worshipped.

He was Shaka Zulu.

Dingane

Dingane became the new chief of the Zulu. He promised that the lives of his people would be much happier under his rule and, to help wipe out ugly memories of the past, he built a huge new capital called unGungundlovu, The Place of the Great Elephant. But his promises were hollow. Dingane turned out to be a cruel and treacherous king who murdered his brother Mhlangana and ordered the murder of Piet Retief and his party of Voortrekkers. He was eventually killed by the Nwayo tribe, after fleeing to Swaziland.

Shaka's place in history

There is no doubt that Shaka was a bloodthirsty tyrant. He was also a brilliant military leader who, in the space of just under twelve years, increased his army from a mere handful of five hundred men to an invincible fifty thousand. Under his leadership, the small Zulu clan became a powerful nation, which stretched from the Indian ocean in the east to the Drakensberg in the west. He taught them obedience and discipline, and was always striving for knowledge and the wisdom to uplift his people and improve their way of life.

Shaka had a very unpredictable temperament and his reign was one of bloodshed and fear. He could be kind and gentle one minute and brutally cruel the next. Nevertheless, he was the undisputed founder of the Zulu nation, and a man who will always have a special place in the history of this country.

SHAKA'S REALM

Lake Sibayi

Pongola River

Mkuze River

Mkuze River

KHUMALO

Zwide's kraal

NDWANDWE

Hluhluwe River

Lake St Lucia

Blood River

White Mfolozi River

Black Mfolozi River

BUTHELEZI

NTOMBELA

ZULU

Mfolozi River

Qokli **Hill battle**

Dingiswayo's kraal

Old Bulawayo kraal

LANGENI

Mfule River

MTHETHWA

DRAKENSBERG

Buffalo River

Mhlatuze River

Tugela River

Mhlatuze river

New Bulawayo kraal

Matigulu

Mlalazi River

INDIAN OCEAN

Pepeta battle

Mool River

QWABE

Tugela River

Mvoti River

Dukuza kraal

Mgeni River

Mdloti River

Mlazi River

Mgeni River

Mkomazi River

Lovu River

Port Natal

DATES AND EVENTS IN SHAKA'S LIFE

1787 Shaka's birth
1793 Shaka and Nandi go to live with the Langeni clan
1803 Nandi sends Shaka to live with the Mthethwa clan
1809 Dingiswayo becomes chief of the Mthethwa clan
1810 Shaka challenges the Buthelezi warrior and Chief Pungashe is defeated
1816 Senzangakhona dies and Shaka takes over as chief of the Zulu and establishes his kraal at Bulawayo
1818 Death of Dingiswayo
1818 Battle of Qokli Hill
1819 The Great Harvest Festival
1819 The second Ndwandwe war
1819 The Great Hunt
1820 The new Bulawayo is built
1821 Shaka's millipede attacks the Pepeta clan
1821 Shaka unifies the Zulu homeland
1822 Attack on the Ranisi clan
1823 Shaka sends a regiment against Mzilikazi and puts him to flight
1824 The great 'smelling out' and the death of Nobela
1824 Fynn and Farewell arrive in Port Natal
1824 Shaka grants Farewell possession of Port Natal
1825 John Ross lands at Port Natal
1826 Death of Mgobozi
1826 Dukuza is built
1827 Death of Nandi
1828 Country released from mourning for Nandi
1828 Shaka assassinated at Dukuza in September

INDEX

FURTHER READING

Becker, P. *Path of Blood*. Longmans, London, 1962
Bergh and Bergh. *Tribes and Kingdoms*. Nelson, Cape Town, 1984
Binns, C.T. *Warrior People*. Timmins, Cape Town, 1974
Bulpin, T.V. *Natal and the Zulu Country*. Books of Africa, Cape Town, 1966
Bulpin, T.V. *Shaka's Country*. Timmins, Cape Town, 1952
Elliott, A. *The Zulu*. Struik, Cape Town, 1986
Elliott, A. *Sons of Zulu*. Collins, London, 1978
Gon and Mulholland. *The First Zulu Kings*. Ad Donker, Craighall, 1985
Krige, F.J. *The Social System of the Zulus*. Longman's, London, 1936
McBride, A. *The Zulu War*. Osprey, London, 1976
Mitchison, N. *African Heroes*. Bodley Head, London, 1968
Morris, D. *The Washing of the Spears*. Cape, London, 1966
Perrett, I.L. *Footprints in Time, Natal*. McGraw Hill, Johannesburg, 1971
Ritter, E.A. *Shaka Zulu*. Longman's, London, 1955
Roberts, B. *The Zulu Kings*. Hamilton, London, 1974
Strydom, F.W. *Die Swart Verskrikking*. Perskor, Johannesburg, 1977
West and Morris. *Abantu*. Struik, Cape Town, 1976

Struik Publishers (Pty) Ltd
(a member of The Struik Publishing Group (Pty) Ltd)
Cornelius Struik House
80 McKenzie Street
Cape Town
8001

Registration No. 54/00965/07

First published in hardcover 1987
First published in softcover 1993
10 9 8 7 6 5

Text © Lynn Bedford Hall
llustrations © René Hermans
© Struik Publishers (Pty) Ltd
Edited by Jane-Anne Hobbs
Photoset by McManus Bros (Pty) Ltd, Cape Town
Reproduction by Unifoto, Cape Town
Printed and bound by Kyodo Printing Co. (Pte) Ltd, Singapore

ISBN 1 86825 418 6